Bright
≡Summaries.com

Life as a User

BY GEORGES PEREC

Life as a User

BY GEORGES PEREC

GEORGES PÉREC

FRENCH WRITER

- **Born in 1936 in Paris**
- **Died in 1982 in Ivry-sur-Seine**
- **Some of his works:**
  - *The Things* (1965), novel
  - *The Disappearance* (1969), novel
  - *W or the Memory of Childhood* (1975), story

Born in 1936 to Polish Jewish parents, Georges Pérec was orphaned at the age of 7 (his father died in the war and his mother was deported).

After studying literature, he published his first novel *Les Choses* in 1965, which won the Prix Renaudot. Influenced by Raymond Quencau, he integrated the scientific constraints of OuLiPo, of which he became a member in 1967, into his subsequent writings (the lipogram in *La Disparition* or monovocalism in *Les Revenentes*).

In 1975, he returned to his childhood in *W ou le Souvenir d'enfance*, in which he alternated between autobiography and adventure novels. In 1978, he published *La Vie mode d'emploi*, a work that was ambitious on all levels and which would become his masterpiece.

Apart from his activities as a writer, Georges Pérec was also a talented cruciverbalist.

He died in 1982, leaving behind numerous texts that were published posthumously, thus enriching a body of work in which, through storytelling and the love of language, one can always read the anguish of disappearance.

LIFE AS A USER

TOTAL NOVEL

- **Genre:** novel

- **Reference edition:** *La Vie mode d'emploi*, Paris, Le Livre de poche, 1986, 706 p.

- **1st edition:** 1978

- **Themes:** art, OuLiPo, sociology, novels, inventory, death

A monster novel, *La Vie mode d'emploi* describes in 6 parts and 99 chapters (one per room) the life of the inhabitants of the building located at 11 rue Simon-Crubellier (an imaginary street in the 17th arrondissement of Paris), from 1875 to 1975.

Constructed in the manner of a puzzle, the writing of this book responds to 42 narrative constraints associated with a mathematical model, all set out in very precise specifications in the form of complex tables (constraints, chronology, stories…). For example, the author has created "pairs", bringing together a table and a book, which are supposed to inspire the writing of 10 chapters each.

La Vie mode d'emploi, which took nine years to write, is Georges Pérec's masterpiece. Indeed, with this, or rather these novels, the author demonstrates his incredible mastery of formal constraints which nevertheless leave (and this is the proof of his genius) plenty of room for reading pleasure.

The book won the Prix Médicis in 1978, the year of its publication, and is constantly cited as a reference by a wide range of writers.

SUMMARY

Following the OuLiPo approach of using constraint as a generator of stories, *La Vie mode d'emploi* is the product of a complex system of rules and constraints. Responding in 1978 to questions from Jean-Jacques Brochier (French journalist and editor of the *Magazine littéraire* from 1968 to 2004), Georges Pérec himself noted that "the book has become a veritable story-telling machine, as much for stories that fit into three lines as for others that span several chapters."

Constructed in 99 small chapters (equivalent to the number of rooms in the building), the author tells more than a hundred stories or short novels spread out over a century in *La Vie mode d'emploi* (and which are listed in the appendix: "Reminder of some of the stories told in this book").

Of this ensemble, which only takes on its full meaning in its totality, certain stories dominate, however, because they are those of the main characters: their stay in the building breaks records for longevity and they return in multiple parts of the book, serving as a thread and a chronology for the whole.

Indeed, Serge Valène moved to 11, rue Simon-Crubellier in 1919 and it was in 1925 that he began giving watercolour lessons to his neighbour Bartlebooth. That same year, a lift was installed in the building. Gaspard and Marguerite Winckler moved into the building in 1932, two years after they were married. They immediately met Valène at a dinner party organised by Bartlebooth. Bartlebooth, true to his life's plan, travelled from 1935 to 1955. He invited his neighbours to come and meet him on his yacht between Trieste and Doubrovnik in 1937.

Of course, it is Bartlebooth's mad project that constitutes the richest plot of the novel, since this character decides "in the face of the inextricable incoherence of the world, [...] to accomplish to the end a programme, limited no doubt, but whole, intact, irreducible" (p. 156). He made this decision when he was just twenty years old, and this programme occupied him until he was seventy-five. Indeed, from the age of twenty-five to thirty-five he decided to take up watercolour painting, and then spent the next twenty years travelling the world and painting landscapes which he sent to Winckler to be transformed into a puzzle. In 1955, he began a new period of twenty years devoted to reconstituting these 500 puzzles before systematically destroying them so that, and this is the whole point of this project, no trace remains of this operation to which he will have dedicated his entire life. Unfortunately, in spite of Bartlebooth's great rigour, several grains of sand slip through the gears of this perfect plan. First of all, he underwent a cataract operation in 1973 and his eyesight gradually deteriorated. However, he managed to overcome this handicap and continued to implement his programme. Similarly, he ignored the offer of Beyssandre, the agent of a patron of the arts who had commissioned him to build up the richest private collection of living painters. To achieve this goal, the agent offers to buy his remaining fragmented watercolours from Bartlebooth for ten million dollars. When this offer is rejected, it is finally the "long revenge that [Gaspard Winckler] has so patiently, so painstakingly wrought" (p. 22) that will cause Bartlebooth to stumble at the gates of his project. A project that he tries to complete with his last breath, since after learning of the death of the cameraman in charge of filming the destruction of the 438th puzzle, his own death surprises him while he is in the process of completing his 439th puzzle.

Around this story, which we could describe as extraordinary, many other intrigues take place, linked to the different inhabitants of the building. The author's ambition being, as he put it, "to exhaust reality," he does not fail to inform us of many details of everyday life. Indeed, according to him: "What really happens, what we live, the rest, everything else, where is it? What happens every day and what comes back every day, the banal, the everyday, the obvious, the common, the ordinary, the infra-ordinary, the background noise, the habitual, how can we account for it, how can we question it, how can we describe it" (*L'Infra-ordinaire*, 1989).

CHARACTER STUDY

GASPARD WINCKLER

The novel opens with a visit from an estate agent who is in charge of the inventory of fixtures of the flat of this character, who died two years before, without leaving any family behind. Various episodes of his life are recounted throughout the book, allowing us to better understand his life. We learn that at the age of 19, Gaspard Winckler, with no ties and no professional career, had enlisted and spent 18 months "not far from Spanish Morocco, where he had practically nothing to do but carve exaggeratedly worked skittles for three quarters of the garrison" (p. 311). Just back from Africa, in 1930, he met Marguerite in Marseilles, who was to become his wife and with whom he settled at 11 rue Simon-Crubellier. Many years after this move, and after losing his wife, he was hired by Bartlebooth to make puzzles. Once this job was finished, in 1955, he started making rings, and then devoted himself to "witch mirrors," stopping all activity two years before his death. He was a solitary man, and one of his only occupations was to go for walks in the Parc Monceau, which he eventually gave up. He only went out for lunch at Riri's and to play backgammon with his neighbour, the chemist Morellet (games that could send him into a frenzy, the man who was so calm) before he died on 29 October 1973.

MARGUERITE WINCKLER

Gaspard's wife, she worked for a collector of antique musical instruments who employed her for her decorative skills. She then worked on her own as a miniaturist. She is a very precise woman who "paradoxically had an irresistible attraction for clutter" (p. 309), as the description of her table shows. She is a "gentle, laughing woman who looked at the world with such clarity" (p. 310). She often walks with her neighbour, the drawing teacher Valène, who eventually confesses his love for her. Through his eyes, we learn that "she was discreetly pretty: a pale complexion dotted with freckles, slightly hollow cheeks, grey-blue eyes" (p. 309). She died "in November nineteen forty-three, giving birth to a still-born child." (p. 313).

SERGE VALÈNE

Serge Valène is a painter. Born in Étampes, he started renting his maid's room on the 7th floor of the building when he arrived in Paris at the age of 19 to attend the Ecole des Beaux-Arts. He never left it and died in 1975, having become the dean of the building. Chapter LI is devoted to an inventory of this room, located above Gaspard Winckler's studio, and of the works that shaped Valène. The artist gave painting lessons and taught watercolour to Bartlebooth for ten years. He never left his room, where he died in 1975. He was very close to Winckler and was secretly in love with his wife, Marguerite. He met the couple a few days after they moved into Bartlebooth's house, who invited the three of them to dinner. Shortly before his death, which follows closely on Barblebooth's death, he had conceived a plan for a 'total' painting that would depict the whole building, including himself (Chapter LI). However, when he is found dead, "The canvas was practically blank: a few carefully drawn charcoal lines divided it into regular squares, a sketch of a cross-sectional plan of a building that no figure would henceforth inhabit" (p. 602).

BARTLEBOOTH

Born in 1900 and died in 1975, his name is constructed from two surnames: Bartelby, a character imagined by the American writer Herman Melville, and Barnabooth, Valery Larbaud's literary double. A wealthy man, he has a valet, Smautf, as well as a chauffeur, a cook, a kitchen girl, a sommelier, a linen maid, a groom, and a footman. To "everyone in the building, [he is] the very symbol of British phlegm, discretion, courtesy, politeness, exquisite urbanity" (p. 418). His drawing room is full of wonders (see Chapter LXXXVII), but as "money, power, art, women did not interest Bartlebooth. Nor science, nor even games" (p. 157), he sets up a project to which he decides to devote his life, following a very precise programme. First of all, and for ten years, he learns the art of watercolour. He took lessons with Valène, and this is how he discovered the building and bought a flat there when he was not yet 30 years old. For the next twenty years, he travelled the world to paint five hundred seascapes (according to a well-rehearsed mechanism described on pages 80 to 84) which he sent to Winckler, so that he could transform them into a puzzle. Finally, for another twenty years, he reconstitutes the puzzles and then destroys them. To do this, he returns to live at 11 Rue Simon-Crubellier, where the inhabitants see him wearing "his usual grey flannel trousers, a checked jacket, and one of those Scottish thread shirts he was so fond of" (p. 166). He refuses the proposals of Beyssandre, a collector, who wants to buy his fragmented watercolours from him at a high price, and dies before he has completed his entire project, a piece of the puzzle in his hand.

THE OTHER INHABITANTS

There are of course many other characters who could be mentioned, since more than 2000 people are involved in *Life in the Workplace*. However, we will only mention the most important ones.

Hortense, "a hard-faced, worried-eyed woman in her thirties" (p. 237) is a pop singer. She became successful by changing her gender and leaving behind the years she lived as Sam Horton.

Gregoire Simpson is fired from his job in a library due to a reduction in staff. Following this dismissal, he began to wander around Paris, his attention focused on a thousand objects, and then, losing his bearings, he ended up shutting himself away in the room he occupied in the building. "Despite the sound of his name, Gregoire Simpson was not in the least English. He came from Thonon-les-Bains. (p. 307).

The Danglars are a couple of magistrates whose sexual perversion consists in committing robberies. They were arrested "on 5 January while trying to think clandestinely in Switzerland. And it was learned with amazement that the high magistrate and his wife had committed, since the end of the war, about thirty burglaries, each more daring than the last." (p. 491).

We also meet **Fernand de Beaumont**, the archaeologist and friend of Bartlebooth who committed suicide on 12 November 1935, leaving behind a wife, Vera, and his "six-year-old daughter, Elizabeth, who had never seen her father, who was away from Paris on his digs" (p. 39).

KEYS TO READING

LA VIE MODE D'EMPLOI, OULIPIEN BOOK

OuLiPo or Ouvroir de Littérature Potentielle was created in 1960 by François Le Lionnais (French engineer and mathematician, 1901-1984) and Raymond Queneau (French writer, 1903-1976). This group, which brought together literary and scientific personalities, set itself the goal of experimenting with various literary constraints (including the abécédaire, the lipogramme, the palindrome, the drawn sonnet, etc.).

At monthly meetings, the members engage in stylistic exercises, or even create new ones, but also analyse older works for which the authors have used, more or less consciously, constraints. These authors are referred to as 'anticipatory plagiarists'.

Among the outstanding works that came into being thanks to OuLiPo, we can cite: Raymond Queneau's *Cent mille milliards de poèmes*, based on the principle of combinatorial poetry, *La Disparition, the* famous lipogramme ('missing a letter', in this case the e) by Georges Pérec, and *La Vie mode d'emploi* by the same author.

The Terms of Reference of La Vie mode d'emploi

For *La Vie mode d'emploi*, Georges Pérec thus applied the system of constraint instituted by OuLiPo. Although he was a great user of it, his talent was above all to make it almost invisible in his texts. In this approach, he was especially interested in the way in which the exercise could be a generator of writing. Indeed, when reading the work, the constraint is invisible, underlying, and therefore does not weigh on the reader in any way. While some may enjoy detecting, under the multiplicity of stories, the constraint that brought them to life, others will be free to simply let themselves be carried away by the pure pleasure of reading. Especially since for *La Vie mode d'emploi*, the constraints are multiple and very sophisticated. Indeed, the specifications that governed the writing of the text are rich and complex. It took the author ten years to complete the book, the idea for which was born of a letter sent to him by another member of OuLiPo, Claude Berge, about the recent discovery of the "orthogonal Latin bi-square of order 10". This grid and its complex distribution system, associated with the polygraphy of the knight (from the game of chess), are at the origin of the structure of the work, the construction of which will follow this wandering through the different rooms of the building.

Constraint as a Generator of Writing and Stories

Georges Pérec's first objective was to take an interest in the lives of the inhabitants of a building. All that remained was to arrange this 'visit' that the reader is invited to make, jumping from one room to another, from one character to his neighbour, from one story to the next. In order for this treasure hunt to be rich and interesting, Pérec has created a sort of "data bank" which constitutes the second constraint of the book. Once again, the specifications shed a great deal of light on his way of doing things, since we have access to the 420 elements, organised in groups of 10, which the author will use to enrich his text. He himself explained in an interview with Jean-Jacques Brochier in 1978: "At the beginning, I had 420 elements, distributed in groups of ten: names of colours, numbers of characters per room, events such as America before Columbus, Asia in Antiquity or the Middle Ages in England, details of furniture, literary quotations, etc. All this provided me with a kind of background for my work. All this provided me with a kind of framework [...]. In each chapter, some of these elements had to fit. That was my kitchen, a scaffolding that took me almost two years to build." Once this framework was in place, Georges Pérec could then move on to the finishing touches for the entire work.

GEORGES PÉREC, BUILDER OF NOVELS

If Proust claims to have built his work as a cathedral, Pérec's choice was for a building... He presented his project in 1974 in *Espèces d'Espaces*: "I imagine a Parisian building whose façade has been removed [...] so that, from the ground floor to the attic, all the rooms in the façade are instantly and simultaneously visible". This six-storey Parisian building is located at 11 rue Simon-Crubellier – an imaginary street in the 17th arrondissement – and is populated by numerous inhabitants, each with a story that, like a puzzle, only makes sense within the system (i.e. the building). The scattered elements, constituted by the short novels of various genres and registers, acquire their full meaning and legibility when put together.

In this respect, Pérec is part of a modern literary trend, since his approach goes against the methods prevailing in the previous century. In fact, the 19th century had accustomed us to individual trajectories (as could have been the case in Guy de Maupassant's *Une vie* or Gustave Flaubert's *Madame Bovary*), whereas here, existence only has meaning in relation to the whole in which it is embedded. The most ordinary existences – for Pérec looks at the infra-ordinary life of the building – acquire a resonance, an importance within this total novel which cannot, by definition, do without the smallest lives. And to summon these lives, Pérec uses enumerations that are longer than the others, which end up resembling an attempt to exhaust reality (wasn't his previous book entitled *Tentative d'épuisement d'un lieu parisien*?). This desire is present in the very text of *La Vie mode d'emploi*, taken over by Bartlebooth whose "desire would be, to describe, to exhaust, not the totality of the world – a project that only its statement is enough to ruin – but a fragment constituted of it." (p. 156)

In doing so, the descriptions of most places seem to be inspired by the pictorial technique of hyperrealism. As might be the case in the New Novel, the characters have no particular psychology, they come to life through their actions or the description of their interiors and what is inside. This total novel is therefore very referential. Indeed, many masterpieces from various arts (painting, literature) are quoted to paint the portrait of the different characters. But once again, it is Pérec's talent not to make these references overwhelming for the reader.

PERCIVAL BARTLEBOOTH, PIVOT OF THE WORK

At the centre of this galaxy of individual destinies is Percival Bartlebooth. A wealthy man with no particular desires, he has dedicated his life to the implementation of a project whose outcome consists of nothing less than his own annihilation. In fact, he has set himself a three-stage programme: ten years to learn the art of watercolour, twenty to paint five hundred seascapes and have them transformed into a jigsaw puzzle, and another twenty to reconstitute them before making them disappear completely. A committed artist, he set himself the objective that "No trace, therefore, [should remain] of this operation which, for fifty years, would have entirely mobilised its author." (p. 158). How then can we not draw a parallel between this plan of extreme constraints, of which the figure of the puzzle is the central element, and the one followed by the author in his writing? Pérec himself envisages his work in this way, since he writes in 1974, in *Espèces d'espaces*: "The whole book was constituted like a house whose pieces would be arranged like those of a puzzle."

Indeed, the book contains, from beginning to end, several references to the puzzle. First of all in its functioning as a puzzle, where each element draws its meaning from the whole in which it fits. Secondly, the puzzle is at the very heart of the plot since it links the main characters of *La Vie mode d'emploi* (Valène the painter, Winckler the craftsman and Bartlebooth the artist, three sides of the same author's mirror). And how can we not read a metaphor for the craft of writing in this description of the art of the puzzle?

> *"From this we shall deduce something that is undoubtedly the ultimate truth of the puzzle: despite appearances, it is not a solitary game: every gesture that the jigsaw artist makes, the jigsaw maker has made before him; every piece that he picks up and picks up again, that he examines, that he caresses, every combination that he tries and tries again, every trial and error, every intuition, every hope, every discouragement, has been decided, calculated, studied by the other."* (p. 251)

The character of Bartlebooth is more than the pivot of the book, he is its very condition, since *La Vie mode d'emploi* ends as soon as he breathes his last, that famous "twenty-third of June nineteen hundred and seventy-five", when it is almost eight o'clock in the evening. The repetition of the date and time serves to introduce the description of all the activities in the building at that exact moment: Kléber is making a success, Mademoiselle Crespi is sleeping, Madame Marcia in her room is opening a jar of Russian pickles… and "an estate agent comes to visit the flat occupied by Gaspard Winckler late at night" (p. 599). So here we are, back in the first chapter of the work, when everything will soon disappear, at the very moment of Bartlebooth's death. The death of the character thus seems to contain all the worlds, he who "wanted the whole project to close in on itself without a trace, like a sea of oil closing in on a drowning man, he wanted nothing, absolutely nothing to remain of it, to emerge only as emptiness, the immaculate whiteness of nothing, the gratuitous perfection of the useless." (p. 481).

Another disturbing detail that seems to make this character the perfect double of his author is the puzzle piece he holds in his hand at the time of his death, which "has the shape, long predictable in its very irony, of a W" (p. 600). This letter obviously refers us to Georges Pérec's book, *W ou le souvenir d'enfance*, a cross-cutting narrative in which the author recounts his painful childhood marked by the loss of his parents (his father died in combat in 1940 and his mother was deported to Auschwitz). This disappearance will never cease to haunt and nourish Pérec's work as a whole.

AVENUES FOR REFLECTION

A FEW QUESTIONS FOR FURTHER REFLECTION...

- "I am looking for the eternal and the ephemeral at the same time", writes Georges Pérec in *Les Revenentes*. How is this quote relevant to La Vie mode d'emploi?

- The character of Grégoire Simpson echoes another work by Georges Pérec, which one?

- It has been said that *La Vie mode d'emploi* is a critique of consumer society.

- What are the different genres used by Pérec in this work?

- In what way can *La Vie mode d'emploi* be considered an autobiographical enterprise?

- What constraints of OuLiPo were used by Pérec in his other works?

- What characteristics does *La Vie mode d'emploi* borrow from the New Novel?

- Disappearance is a recurring theme in Pérec's work. How does it operate in *La Vie mode d'emploi*?

- Pérec's writing always combines tragedy and humour, give examples from *Life's Way*.

TO GO FURTHER

REFERENCE EDITION

PÉREC Georges, *La Vie mode d'emploi*, Paris, Le Livre de Poche, 1986.

BENCHMARK STUDIES

OuLiPo website: http://oulipo.net/

PÉREC Georges, *Espèces d'espaces*, Paris, éditions Galilée, 1974.

PÉREC Georges, *W ou le souvenir d'enfance*, Paris, Denoël, 1975.

PÉREC Georges, *L'Infra-ordinaire*, Paris, Le Seuil, 1989.

CHUNG Ye Yung, *The building, the empty box, the novel*, Literature No. 139, 2005.

COLLECTIVE, *Georges Pérec*, Éditions Incultes, 2005.

Your opinion is important to us!
Leave a comment on the website of your online bookshop
and share your favourites on social networks!